LONNIE TENTATON

Copyright 2008
ISBN 0-9713409-3-5

EAGLE POINT PUBLISHING CO.
108 MADISON ST., ST. LOUIS MO 63102

In the heart of southeastern Missouri, at the edge of the Ozark Mountains, lies the little town of Clayville, Missouri. It was a typical Midwestern town in the 1960s. The shoe factory closed due to foreign competition. The glass factory was still going strong. The surrounding small towns were holding their own.

In the mid-sixties there were a lot of social and economic changes taking place. It was the beginning of the electronic age. Transistor radios and computers were starting to take hold. However, they were very expensive and complicated to the average person. The Vietnam War was questioned by the youth.

The Botz family consisted of Leonard Junior and his wife Lillian. They had two sons and one daughter. Leonard requested that all family members' names start with the letter "L". The sons' names were Leon and Leroy and the daughter's name was Lou Ann. At the time the story begins, Leon and Leroy were two middle-aged men trying to maintain a struggling business. Their father had passed away and their mother was 93.

The Botz Bros.

Leon

Leroy

Leon was a prankster, always fun loving and happy.

Leroy was serious, a strictly business type man.

Their sister Lou Ann went to Southeastern Missouri State University. She met and married a wealthy classmate and moved to Los Angeles, California. The last thing she said to Leon was, "I'm glad to get out of this one horse, hick town."

The Botz brothers' task was struggling to keep the failing family business alive and turn it around. Just before he died, their mother promised their father that the business would continue to operate.

The Botz Bottling Company started in Clayville in 1905. It was famous for its root beer.

Leonard Sr. had a root beer concession stand at the 1904 World's Fair in St. Louis, Missouri. The root beer was served from a large keg surrounded by ice. The large glass mugs the root beer was served in were kept in another wooden keg filled with ice. Leonard's own formula and the ice cold root beer was a huge success in that sweltering summer of 1904.

With his earnings from the Fair, Leonard started Botz Bottling Company. It was very successful in mid and southwestern Missouri towns.

Lou Ann Botz. A Cheerleader at SEMO.

The Botz First Woody Station Wagon

The Second Botz Woodie
The Wood Grain Effect Was Metal.
Lou Ann And Leroy
Arrive Home From School.
Leon Chose To Walk Home.
What Mischief Could He Get Into?

CHAPTER 1

Leon was a prankster even at a young age. Leon and Leroy were in church with their mother one Sunday morning. Leon loudly farted. A strong odor wafted through the air. In a loud whisper, Leon said, "Leroy, ewww, P.U." Lillian gave Leroy a mean look. As they left church, their mother grabbed Leroy, jerked him aside and started to beat him. "But mother," Leroy cried. Lillian said, "Don't ever do that in church again!" Leon was off to the side snickering.

On another Sunday afternoon, Leon and Leroy were at their Aunt Polly's with their parents. Aunt Polly often invited them over for a chicken dinner. Leroy found a rare frog down by the creek. It had a bright yellow and green pattern on its back. Leroy was sitting on the steps playing with it and showing it to everyone who walked in front of the porch. Aunt Polly always kept a pitcher of iced tea on the front porch railing. Leroy turned around to pet the old hound dog lying next to him and Leon hurriedly picked up the frog and put it in the pitcher of iced tea. Then he slipped around to the side of the house. At that time Aunt Polly came out of the house, saw the frog in the tea, and screamed. Lillian came out to see what was wrong. Aunt Polly said, "Leroy put that frog in my tea." Lillian grabbed Leroy and started to spank him. Leroy said, "But, Mother." She said, "Leroy, it's your frog."

Leroy, two years older than Leon, caught up with him, grabbed him by the collar, and pulled him close and said, "One of these days I'm going to knock you on your butt!"

TUTTATON

CHAPTER 2

Leon's buddy Pete thought that Leon's pranks were funny, even if the joke was on him. The two were good friends through grade school and high school. In grade school they were in Mrs. Tetlow's class. They sat near the back of the room. Leon sat next to Bobby, and Pete sat on the other side of Bobby. They were always putting things in each other's seat. Items included dead lizards, pine cones, water, glue and dried dog poop. Pete would draw humorous caricatures of Mrs. Tetlow using puns with her name. Including one picture which he labeled "Mrs. Titlow". He put it on Bobby's desk for Mrs. Titlow to find. She found it, and Pete and Leon had a good laugh.

Pete's artistic abilities were not limited to drawing pictures. When Pete got older, he painted names on his friends' cars. He also painted a few signs. But Pete was proudest of his '39 Ford Coupe. He gave it a nice deep red paint job — it impressed all the guys and gals in town.

Early one summer evening, Pete was trying to impress his girlfriend with his newly painted car. Leon followed Pete and his girlfriend Cindy at a distance to the Black River. Pete parked on a small ridge back from the river's edge. While Pete and Cindy were throwing rocks into the river and playing around on the river's edge, Leon was at work. While the sun was setting, Leon finished his work. Just before darkness fell, Pete and Cindy returned to the car. Pete started the car, put it in reverse, and pressed on the gas. The engine raced, but the car didn't move. Pete's mind was racing as fast as his engine. "Oh no, did my transmission go out? Maybe it's the rear end." He got out and looked at the back tires. As soon as he stepped out of the car he heard Leon's unmistakable laugh coming from behind the trees nearby. Leon had jacked Pete's car up and placed blocks under the axle. When he let the jack down it left the tires about one inch off the ground. Leon helped Pete get the blocks out from under the car. Leon, Pete, and

Cindy laughed for ten minutes. They all three enjoyed a good joke, even if it was on them.

While still in high school, the Botz brothers went to work in the family bottling business. Their father taught them all aspects of the business. They handled everything from delivery, to bottling, to supply. The one thing their father couldn't show them was the maintenance end of it. That is where Uncle Mike came in. Uncle Mike worked for Botz Bottling Company off and on for twenty years. Uncle Mike was not really anyone's uncle but that's what everyone called him. The boys loved Uncle Mike's sense of humor and could listen to his stories for hours.

Uncle Mike's stories usually had large families in them. Maybe a big family was something missing in his life.

One of Uncle Mike's stories was about being from a large, poor family. He said, "There were 10 kids in my family. We were so poor we couldn't afford to put cheese in the mousetrap. My little sister drew a picture of some cheese, colored it, and put it in the mousetrap. Guess what? We caught a picture of a mouse."

When little children came around to talk to Uncle Mike, he would say, "Let me tell you the story of my life. I was born at a very young age without a stitch of clothes on my back. I was born in a barn at midnight. There were five bright stars over in the east. Three battalions from the 333rd Army came riding up the hill on donkeys to see me. They believed I was to be their new leader. The five stars meant that I was to be a five-star general. Well, I ended up in the Navy. I had often thought of going back, if they would give me my old rank back as Admiral of the fleet." The military story may have gone over some of the kids heads, but they still loved the story.

One of their favorite stories was of a hunter named Jake, who was the fastest runner anyone had ever seen. Jake never had to shoot rabbits. He just chased them down and hit them with a club. He told another story about how Jake had a gun that shot little iron balls. He saw a deer getting a drink of water at a stream. He figured he would shoot the deer, then run up and grab the deer by the tail before it fell into the stream. Jake shot the deer then ran so fast that when he reached the deer, the iron ball hit him in the back of the head, knocking them both in the water and the deer got away.

Uncle Mike had a great personality and was fun to be around, most of the time. The only problem with Uncle Mike was he drank too much. He would work hard for two weeks and then drink for a week. He was easy to get along with until his third or fourth day into his drinking, and then he would get obnoxious. When he got to that state, no one wanted to be around him.

Even though Mike had a drinking problem, he could always find work. He worked at places like the bottling plant, Shelly's parent's farm, the hardware store, and the feed store. He always worked hard and did a good job. Everyone that he would work for knew he was good for two weeks worth of hard work, then he would be gone.

Mike had a three-legged dog that was with him all the time. No matter what, his dog Limpy always stuck with him.

After work, Uncle Mike liked to sit around and play folk tunes on his guitar and entertain anyone who happened to be around.

One of Uncle Mike's stories was about when he was a little boy. He was from a family of five children raised by their mother. His mother called all the kids together and announced that she had invited their granny over for supper and she wanted the kids to behave themselves and act like they had some manners at the supper table. She reminded them to use their fork, not to reach across the table and ask for food to be passed. "I don't want her to think I'm raising a bunch of heathens."

When granny arrived for supper, everyone sat down at the table. Everything was going fine. There was one pork chop left on the platter in the middle of the table. No one made a move for the pork chop. Suddenly the lights went out. There was a loud screech, and then the lights came back on. There were six forks sticking in Granny's hand.

Uncle Mike never drove. He walked everywhere. Nothing was too far away. When Leon saw Mike walking, he would stop and give him and his three-legged dog a ride. Mike always had a one-liner joke to tell like, "Did you hear about the cannibal who passed his brother in the woods?" or "A good Marine never leaves their buddies behind," or "Life dealt me a bad hand, until I discovered I was the dealer." "The toes you step on today, may be attached to the ass you have to kiss tomorrow."

Some of Uncle Mike must have rubbed off on Leon. In many ways their mannerisms were the same.

Maybe listening to all of Uncle Mike's stories inspired Leon and many of his friends to join the Army Reserves. The unit was in Marston, a neighboring town. This gave them a little extra money each month.

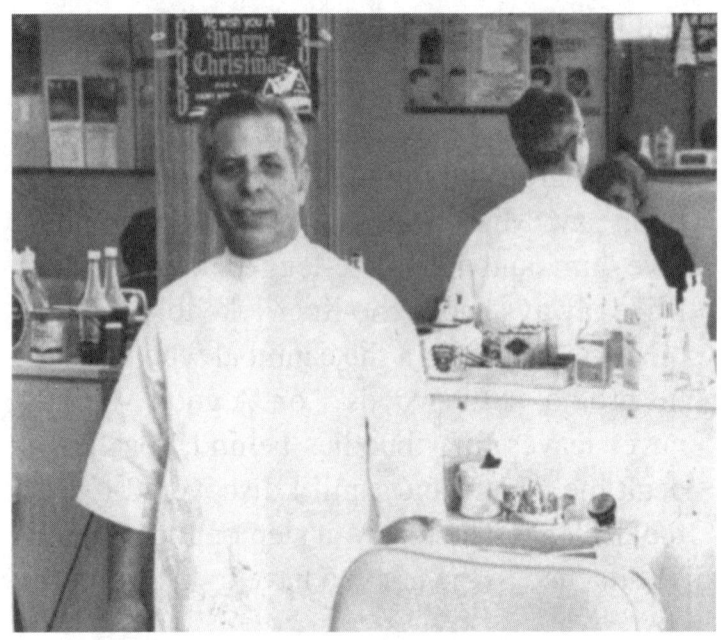

Uncle Mike's brother, Jerry, was the town barber. He was very popular with the townspeople. He took a trip to Las Vegas one summer and was killed after he fell asleep at the wheel and crashed into a ravine on his trip home.

Uncle Mike enjoyed telling stories and playing folk songs, he had no problem finding an audience. The youth of the town especially loved him.

A lonely man with many many friends. Everyone in town knew him.

CHAPTER 3

Leonard Botz was trying to find a gimmick for selling the root beer. While the boys were still in high school, Leroy and Leonard came up with the idea of the dancing bottle. The bottle frame was made of light balsa wood shaped like a soda bottle. It was big enough for a person to fit inside. The bottle framework was covered with canvas and a lacquer finish. The bottom was open so the dancer's legs were free to maneuver.

There was a shoulder harness built inside to hold the bottle weight. There was also a lever built inside to control the bottle cap. The girl inside could flip the bottle cap open at will. There was a slit in the front of the bottle for the girl to see out. It looked like part of the label.

Leroy started dating Shelly, the Botz bottle girl. They met in high school. Their father, Leonard Jr., chose Shelly to be the bottle girl because she was the daughter of Bill Green, a friend of his. She attended dancing school, had the lead in the high school musical, and had great legs, especially at her young age. Bill was happy to escort his daughter to all the Botz Bottling events.

The dancing bottle went over big at picnics and fairs in southwestern Missouri. The dancing bottle helped sell soda.

CHAPTER 4

Pete became a sign painter while he was still in high school. Each summer an old sign painter named Lonnie Tettaton from St. Louis, came to Clayville. Lonnie would go right to work and spend two to three weeks painting signs for Botz Bottling Company. The signs he painted were called privilege signs. The signs were painted on the side walls of buildings and on storefronts. Leonard Jr. would have the customer's name painted on the sign if they would allow a Botz ad to be painted on the building. This worked well for both parties.

Pete took an interest in sign painting. He was fascinated by Lonnie's work and followed him around asking questions. Lonnie took Pete on as a helper. He liked Pete and taught him everything he could about the sign trade. During the winter months, Lonnie sent Pete books on sign painting and supplies so he could practice. After two years of training Pete, Lonnie turned the Botz account over to him. When the old-timer left Clayville for the last time he had a long talk with Pete. As he sat in the front seat of his truck with the door open, "Lad, you have talent and you're ambitious. You are ready to be on your own." He lit his pipe, slapped Pete on the shoulder, and slowly drove off into the sunset.

The Botz Bottling Plant

The Botz Home

CHAPTER 5

Leroy graduated high school two years before Leon. Leroy went to work for the bottling company right out of high school. He handled most of the business affairs because his father was in poor health at that time.

Leroy married Shelly. She was a beautiful bride. Everyone was proud of Leon for restraining himself at the wedding and reception (no pranks).

Leon had just started to work full time at the plant. The Botz bottle had an appearance at a church picnic in Springdale. Leon smeared part of a rotten egg inside the bottle. Leroy helped Shelly in the bottle. She started dancing and the foul odor hit her. The stench was so terrible that it caused her to vomit inside the bottle. She stopped dancing and exited the bottle. Leroy knew immediately that Leon had pulled another prank. Leroy was very angry. He screamed at Leon, "You idiot! One of these days I'm going to knock you on your ass! She happens to be pregnant."

For the first time, Leon apologized for his actions. He felt so bad. He repeatedly apologized to Leon and Shelly. He asked if he could take them to dinner to make up for his mistake. Shelly said, "If I eat anything I'll just throw up, but thank you, maybe some other time."

CHAPTER 6

Life began to get serious for the Botz brothers. Leon came home one day to discover his father's health had taken a turn for the worse. The doctor was there and he told Leon and Lillian that Leonard may not live another 24 hours. It was discovered that Leonard had colon cancer. The doctor caught it too late. Leon called the florist over in Marston and had them deliver flowers to Shelly and his mother. The flowers arrived just before Leroy and Shelly arrived. They thought it was so sweet to get flowers from Leon.

Shortly after Leroy and Shelly arrived, Betty, a girl that Leon had been dating showed up. They were all glad to see her. Betty was concerned and stayed with them. Their sister Lou Ann and her husband Jim got there a little later that evening from Los Angeles. They flew into St. Louis, then rented a car, to complete their trip. The family sat up all night; no one said much of anything. Lillian and the doctor stayed in the room with Leonard during his last hours. The doctor came into the room, followed by Lillian, and said Leonard passed away at 2:15 a.m. It was on a Sunday morning. They hugged each other and there was a feeling of closeness that the family had never experienced before. Leon and Betty hugged each other tightly. It was like an emerging love between them. Leon discovered that for the first time in his life he was in love. This feeling of love between them was so strong, they didn't want to leave each others side. At the crack of dawn, Pete came by to give his condolences. He loved Leonard like his own father. Uncle Mike stopped by later that evening. He felt such gratitude to Leonard for being able to work at the bottling company for so many years. When he found out about Leonard's death he went on a drinking binge. When he arrived at the Botz residence, he was so drunk they put him to bed to sleep it off.

    The funeral was held on Tuesday. The church was packed for the service. Lillian was a strong woman and she took it all well. Leon was still living at home so he could watch after Lillian, although, she was quite capable of taking care of herself.

Two days after they buried Leonard, Leon got a notice that they were calling up his reserve unit to go to Korea. This was serious. The United States was involved in a conflict between North and South Korea. They called it a police action, not a war. There were sure a lot of battles taking place no matter what they called it. The unit was given five days to get their affairs in order. In just five days, Leon was going to have to leave his true love. On his last night at home, Leon proposed to Betty. She answered, "Yes! Yes!" before he could finish. They didn't have much time to make plans, but they had their dreams for the future. They both knew he would be coming back no matter what.

At 10:00 a.m. Monday, the train was leaving. It was a sad day in Clayville. It was like the youth of the entire town were leaving. How many would not be coming back? The soldiers from the surrounding areas gathered at the depot in Marston. As the train pulled away, the tears started to fall. This was a sad day for the mothers. They saw their husbands off to World War II, now they were seeing their sons off to Korea.

Leon's unit only had to serve eight months. All the boys from Clayville returned safely. Upon Leon's arrival, he married Betty. He joined his brother in the business and started a family.

CHAPTER 7

The years flew by. Leon and Leroy's families were starting to mature. Leroy's girls were 18, 16 and 15. Leon's boys were 16, 15 and 14. The two middle-aged men found themselves in the mid-sixties in a failing business. They were always able to support two families from the business, but it was getting harder each year. The business was starting to fail. Leon and Leroy were trying to figure out ways to shore up the business and turn it around. Leon said, "Soda in cans is becoming very popular. That could be our answer."

Leroy said, "Yes, we need to invest in canning machinery. Maybe the bank will loan us the money we need. Let's go over to the bank and talk to Bobby, the bank president.

Leon replied, "It would be best if you went alone. You are better at that stuff than me."

Leroy scheduled a meeting with Bobby at the bank and presented his proposal. Why he needed the money and how it would be used.

With a half serious and half revengeful look on his face, Bobby gave his answer. "You know Leroy, if it was just you, I think it would be okay, but I can't stand that brother of yours. I won't back anything if that clown of a brother of yours is involved. I wouldn't lend him a dime. When we were in Mrs. Tetlow's class, Leon and Pete sat by me. Pete slapped me on the back of the head, I said 'hey,' and turned around, then Leon slipped a picture on my desk. Pete must have drawn it. It was a picture of Mrs. Tetlow with a tit hanging out, way low. He wrote on it, 'Miss Titlow.' When she came back to my desk, she blamed me for it. I almost got suspended, and further more," Bobby continued, "he has caused trouble for me again. Leon had one of his Army buddies call me and pretend to be a Los Angeles business man. He said, 'Lou Ann Kelly, you may know her as Lou Ann Botz, from Clayville, recommended you. There is a large development planned for your area. My firm and partners are looking for a local bank to deposit one hundred million dollars. We will be out next week to check out your bank.' Man was I ever happy. It was the shot in the arm we needed. We immediately got busy cleaning and getting things in order. We wanted the bank to look sharp. The next day your damned brother called and said, 'Did you get that one hundred million dollars?' and laughed his silly laugh that gave him away. I did not think it was very funny."

The next morning at the plant, Leroy confronted Leon. "Thanks to your prank on Bobby, he turned us down. One of these days I'm gonna knock you on your ass!"

Leon replied, "Bobby is nothing but a big sissy punk, he always was. Besides, I don't think Mom would have let us get a loan on this building."

Leroy said, "You know, Coke has been moving in on us recently and now with throw-away cans, it's going to hurt more. I understand Pepsi is starting to use throw-away bottles on the East coast. You know Leon, that may be the way to go. Paying a deposit and returning the bottles is a big pain in the ass for most. We could get a good deal from the glass company if we ordered large quantities of glass bottles. We could raise the cost of the soda by a penny. I think people would pay a little more and not have to bother with bottle returns."

Leon smiled and said, "Great idea, let's do it. In another 30 or 40 years we will become a throw away society anyway."

CHAPTER 8

Two of the best and most profitable events of the year for Botz were the Fourth of July picnic and the Washington County Fair. The Fourth of July picnic was sponsored by the Clayville Lion's Club. A good many of the businessmen in town belonged to the Lions Club.

The Botz brothers belonged to the Lions Club. Their father had been a charter member. On the meeting nights, most members got there a little early and relaxed at the bar with a drink. On this one evening Leon casually strolled in to the dining room. The waitresses were back in the kitchen helping get the dinner ready. Leon went to every third table and unscrewed the salt shaker lid then laid it back on top of the shaker. Shortly after, the meeting was called to order. They said the Pledge of Allegiance and a prayer then sat down. The food was served and everyone prepared to eat. Almost simultaneously two members dumped the shaker of salt in their food. At the same time they shouted, "Leon!" Leon turned to Nelda, one of the waitresses, and said, "Nelda, when you filled the salt shakers, why didn't you screw the lids back on tighter." Nelda replied, "Kiss my ass Botz." Leon replied, "Make it bare." Leon was very good at blaming others for his pranks.

The main topic at the meeting was the big Fourth of July picnic which was only four weeks away. Greg Allen, who was the managing partner of KXBX the radio station in Clayville, announced that Ferlin Husky would be coming over from Springfield to make a personal appearance. Another member asked, "How much will that cost us?" "Nothing," Greg replied. "Ferlin is a good friend of mine. I was instrumental in getting his first hit promoted. He owes me big time. *Since You Have Gone* went straight to the top of the country and pop charts. *On the Wings of a Snow White Dove* made him rich." Greg also added that the Lester Family, a famous gospel group from St. Louis would be performing at the picnic. He also announced that the dancing Botz soda bottle would be back after 19 years. Leroy took the floor and explained that his 18-year-old daughter, Linda, would be the new Botz Bottle girl. While he had the floor, Leroy said, "I understand the Springdale Lion's, who have been setting up a concession stand at our picnic for years, will be selling Coke along with their usual hotdogs, cotton candy, and lemonade. How did that happen?" Dale from IGA Market responded, "It's fountain Coke served in paper cups, and I don't see anything wrong with it."

Leon took the floor and replied, "I see something wrong with it; it's cutting into our business. Are you in bed with Coke? I notice that you are running a lot of specials on Coke products. Are you trying to knock Botz and Pepsi right off the shelves?"

Dale responded, "The only thing you have going for you is your root beer. Your other flavors taste like crap!"

Leon stood up and shouted, "Up yours, Dale!"

The president called for order in the meeting and continued, "the purpose of the Lions is to promote eyesight, and personal business should not be brought into a meeting."

Includes the original recordings of:
GONE • WINGS OF A DOVE • JUST FOR YOU • ONCE
EVERY STEP OF THE WAY • I CAN'T STOP LOVING YOU
I FEEL BETTER ALL OVER • MY REASONS FOR LIVING
A DEAR JOHN LETTER • HEAVENLY SUNSHINE
I REALLY DON'T WANT TO KNOW

Leon and Dale told the president they were sorry. The Tail Twister dashed over to Leon and told him he had to pay a .50 fine for saying ass. Leon said, "Your ass too," and dropped .50 in the Tail Twister's can. They both laughed. The meeting continued with a report from the eyesight chairman. "Last year," he stated, "from the proceeds of our picnic, we gave $1,600 to the state eye research center in Columbia and spent $900 for regional charitable organizations and $550 for eye glasses for the needy. Let's keep up the good work fellas."

Occasionally Leon would bring his dry cleaning in a brown paper bag to the meetings. Ralph, a club member, operated a large dry cleaning plant on the town square. People from all over the area went to Ralph's. Ralph would take the clothes to the cleaners and Leon would pick them up there at his convenience. Ralph forgot to take the bag with him. Leon took the clothes to a small cleaners two doors down from the plant.

At the next Lions Club meeting, Leon asked Ralph, "What happened to my dry cleaning? I went to pick it up and it wasn't there." Ralph said, "I'll check it out."

There had been some doubts as to whether Greg could really get Ferlin Husky for the picnic or not. Greg announced that he would definitely be there. This announcement got a big round of applause.

A week passed and another Lions meeting was at hand. Just before the meeting started, Ralph approached Leon and said, "Sorry, but we are going to have to make an insurance claim on your clothes." Leon quietly responded, "I forgot to tell you that I was only kidding about the clothes." Ralph exploded, "You no good rotten bastard, damn you! We turned that place upside down looking for your clothes. I threatened to fire people. I gave my employees all kinds of hell." Leon replied, "I am really sorry. I should have told you. Ralph, you like our root beer? I'll send over a couple of cases tomorrow." Dinner was very quiet. During dessert, Ralph leaned over to Leon and whispered, "You asshole." And they both smiled.

CHAPTER 9

At the plant, the Botz brothers were trying to find ways to boost sales. Leon said maybe they should create a flavor that no one else had. He suggested Pineapple Cherry Cola. Leroy quickly reminded him that all the flavors he already came up with tasted like crap. Leon said, "How about something that looks and sounds like Coke, like Cock Cola. We could have a red label with the big flowing Cs." Leroy responded, "What is the slogan going to be — Things go better with Cock!? That is a terrible idea. Coke would put us out of business." Leon continued to brainstorm ideas. "Maybe we could bottle iced tea — everyone likes iced tea. Leroy discarded the idea. "Have you ever tasted tea after it's been sitting around all day? However, if we could find a way to preserve the flavor and keep it fresh, let's think about it." Leon also suggested bottling water. "I'll bet bottled water would go over big. People are going over to Springdale with gallon jugs to get that natural spring water. It comes out of that mountain clean, cold, and pure. It really tastes good."

"People will never buy bottled water. Why should they pay for it when they can get as much as they want for free?" Leroy responded.

"I think people will buy it for the convenience. It's the coming thing. We are headed for a mobile society. It would be just the thing for travelers, people working in the sun, mountain climbers and hikers. We could get a jump on it," Leon added excitedly.

Leroy decided the best thing to do was to advertise in the county journal and run a special.

Leon remembered that a new bar and liquor store had opened up over in Washington. "Maybe we can work a deal out with them, a small variety store that had been in that location moved and left their signs behind," Leon said.

Leon and Pete went to see the new business owner. The bar owner was running out of start up capital and the only identification he had was a temporary banner. He was happy to work out a co-op with Botz. Washington Liquor would pay half of the sign cost and Botz would pay half. Leon offered to help Pete to defray part of the cost. Leon coated out the old signs to prepare them for Pete. The liquor store got half the space and Botz got an ad on the other half.

On Saturday, the two headed to Washington to do the sign painting. They hadn't had time to spend together lately, they had both been busy. Pete said, "Remember you used to call my little brother Repeat because he looked so much like me? We found that old brownie camera that someone had thrown away. You rolled up a big soggy mud ball. We told Repeat to sit on the steps so we could take his picture. He was sitting up straight with a big smile on his face. You stepped out from around the corner of the house and threw that mud ball at Repeat, hitting him upside the head, knocking him clean off the porch. He went screaming into the house. My mom came screaming out of the house. She was really mad. She gave us both a whipping. She was still digging mud out of Repeat's ear days later. I caught hell for days after that."

Leon said, "Remember when we were Boy Scouts over at Beaumont Scout Reservation. We were full of our tricks. It was our annual camporee. On the first night we had to cook a meal in foil on an open camp fire. The scout master had us put a piece of steak, a potato, a carrot and an onion in the foil. Then we wrapped it and placed it on the hot coals from the fire. There were wild onions growing nearby. I picked some and snuck them into Bob Hake's foil. After everyone ate and was gathered around the campfire, Bob began to get sick. He got so sick the assistant scout master had to take him into town to the doctor. You know he never forgave me. I don't know if it was the onions or something else that made him sick. Anyway, he still holds it against me. He must have really been sick."

Pete responded, "Yeah, the second night we tied knots in the legs of a pair of pants. They were wet and someone hung them over the tent to dry. Did you ever try to get a knot out of something wet?"

They both laughed and Leon said, "We pulled the tent pegs out of half the camp and snuck under the back of our tent, like we didn't know what was going on with two boys in a tent. That was a mess for them both trying to climb out from under the tent at the same time."

Pete and Leon got to the job site and went right to work. They finished the sign painting just before dark. They packed up and headed back to Clayville.

CHAPTER 10

Botz Soda company sponsored a race car. Betty's brother Charlie was the driver. Stock car races were held every Friday night at the Springdale Speedway. Charlie in the Botz stock car was one of the top drivers at the track. His big competition was Max Walters. He and his father owned Walter's Service Station and Garage in Springdale. These two drivers were always battling it out in the feature race. One of them always won, leaving the pack behind. Every year the Springdale Speedway sponsored the Missouri State Stock Car Championship. It ran Saturday and Sunday the first weekend in August. Rusty Wallace and Ken Schraeder from Valley Park, Missouri, came to race. Rusty and Ken always won the state championship. Charlie, in the Botz car, had to settle for second or third. Botz soda and other businesses were big promoters of the event. Fans from all over the state packed into the track stands. The race was good for the economy of the entire area.

Each year Botz soda bought ad space at the track, a sign at the main entrance and on the fence inside the track. When Leon and Leroy had to cut expenses where they could, they decided the stock car had to go. It cost more to support than what it brought in, however, they did keep their sign space at the track. It was a very economical way to advertise.

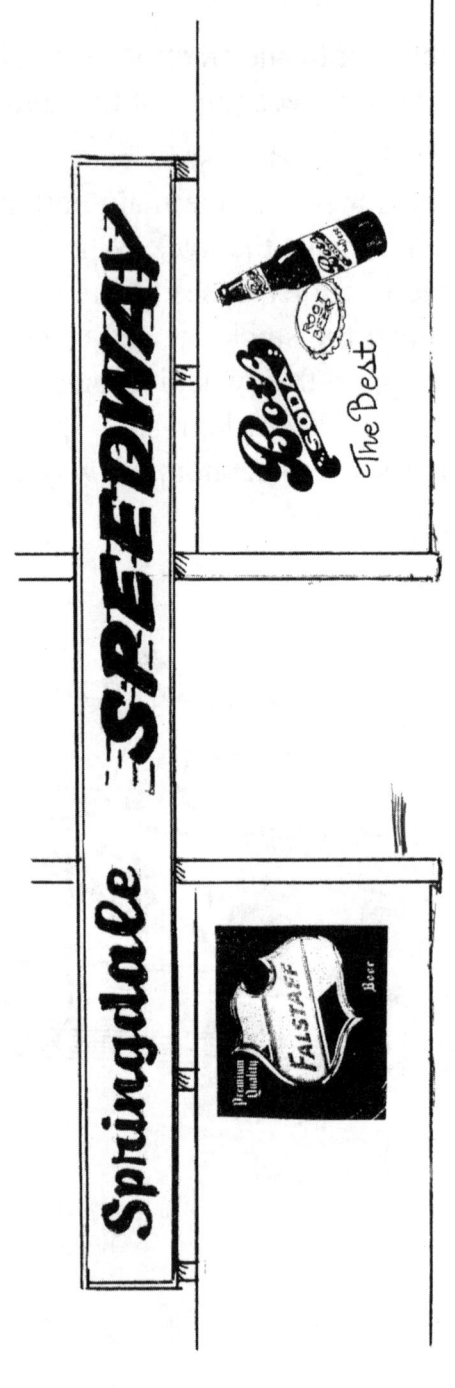

CHAPTER 11

On the third, the Lions Club had all the help they could get to set up for the big day. The Catholic church set up a Chug-A-Lug Wheel, a game of chance. The Presbyterian church had a cake walk. The Baptist church set up a dunking booth. Any organization was welcome to participate. The Lions Club got a percentage of the profit.

The parade started at 10:00 a.m. It included three high school marching bands. The Shriners from Springfield brought three units. A marching bagpipe band was also there. The mounted patrol, on their beautiful horses marched in precision. The motor patrol came over and drove in the parade. They had those small cars and drove in circles, weaving in and out, just missing each other. The Boy Scouts and Girl Scouts marched in the parade. They had clowns and they had Uncle Sam riding on a float throwing candy to the audience. The Lions had a marching band called Junior Lions made up of kids and

Leroy's Daughter Linda The New Botz Bottle Girl Practicing Her Dance Routine.

grand kids of the members. The Botz dancing bottle was always a hit in the parade.

At Shelly's request there were some changes made to the bottle. The interior was changed so there could be a better fan put in and a bigger viewing area was created. They also updated the music that the bottle played when the button was pushed. The melody was catchy and Linda, Leroy's daughter, was to dance a little jig while the song played. The words were — "Botz soda is the best, forget about all the rest, Orange and Cola are divine, you can't find a better Lemon-Lime, try our Grape, Peach, or Cherry. Botz Root Beer is king."

The parade lasted less than an hour. By noon the food was ready. They had every kind of junk food you could think of — snow cones, cotton candy, popcorn, corn dogs, hot-dogs, funnel cakes, and hamburgers. They also had chicken dinners, barbecue ribs, slabs, and sandwiches were available. The event took place at the city park at the edge of town. There were two permanent buildings and several large tents. There was plenty of shady space. A makeshift stage was set up under the larger pavilion. The main entertainment didn't start until evening. Tinsey's Amusements from over in High Hill set up a few carnival rides each year. A local farmer brought a pony for pony rides.

Periodically, throughout the afternoon, there were little attractions taking place. A guy brought a bear for the public to see. The deal was, you paid $2.00 to wrestle the bear. If you were able to pin the bear, you would win $25.00. Pete thought he could pin the bear. He had five minutes to pin the bear with a four-count. The wrestling started with Pete and the bear standing facing each other, with their hands on each others shoulders. Pete stood a head higher than the bear. They wrestled, rolling around on the ground. Pete had the bear on his back ready to pin him, the bear grunted and tossed Pete through the air. While getting up off the ground, Pete shook his body, hands and head, and then said, "Man, that little booger is strong."

One of the other attractions was a guy who blew himself up with six sticks of dynamite.

A couple of pilots that flew crop dusters from the M & L Flying Service made an appearance. Their business was spraying pesticides on the cotton crops in the boot heel area. The planes were especially designed for maneuverability. While spraying they had to be able to pull the plane up sharply at the end of the rows of ten, straight up to avert trees or electric lines. The flyers flew in precision. They flew upside down close to the ground and performed many interesting acrobatic stunts.

The famous Botz Bottle hung around the Botz soda stand. The root beer was iced up in giant kegs and the glass mugs were kept in a cooler. The customers were served root beer in a frosty ice cold mug. The mugs were to be kept near the stand. They had a monitor watching to be sure no one walked off with one. The mugs were collected, washed and put back in the cooler. There was always a crowd around the Botz stand waiting for a frosty, creamy, thirst quenching root beer.

Leon's Son Josh Checking Out A Crop Duster

Ferlin Husky showed up at the picnic in late afternoon. Greg Allen of KXBX radio took him over to meet Leon and Leroy. "Your root beer is the greatest," exclaimed Ferlin, as he shook their hands vigorously. "I love it, but it's getting hard to find in Springfield." The Botz brothers and Ferlin immediately became friends. Leon asked Ferlin if he would do a commercial to endorse Botz Root Beer as he handed him a frosty mug of root beer.

"I only came back home because my mother had a serious operation yesterday and I wanted to be there. If you will meet me over at the station early in the morning, I will cut a couple of commercials for you, then I have to hit the road. The only thing I ask is that you send me a case of Botz Root Beer each month for as long as I live. It was agreed that they would meet at the radio station at 7:00 a.m. the next morning.

A crowd started to gather around the main pavilion. The show started around 8:00 p.m. The show opened with the choir leader of the Baptist church singing "God Bless

America." She sounded just like Kate Smith. It was so beautiful it brought tears to many eyes.

Next to appear was the Lester Family from St. Louis. The twelve members of the group ranged in age from six to seventy. After the Lester Family came the Pilot Knob cloggers, a teenage square dance group. The final entertainer was Ferlin Husky. He sang his two biggest hits, *Since You're Gone* and *On the Wings of a Snow White Dove*.

Thanks to Ferlin, the Lions picnic had the biggest crowd ever. After the show, the crowd was treated to a fireworks display.

The next morning, bright and early, Ferlin recorded the commercials at the station while Leon and Leroy filled his new Lincoln full of Botz Root Beer.

An Added Feature At The Picnic

![Johny K and His Continentals]

Johnny's Band performed from 1953 until 1967. The band members are as follows: (Left to right) — Johnny K., Bass Guitar; Joe Favuzza, Accordion; Fred Beuchner, Accordion; Gertrude Kedro, Piano/Flute; Harold Vondora, Banjo. (Photo, 1965)

CHAPTER 12

In the early 1960s, the Lester family was one of the most famous Gospel groups in the country. It was a big hit at the fourth of July picnic.

Based in St. Louis, the family business was Lester Music Company. The store was on Thirty-Ninth Street, near the south side. The business gave music lessons and sold a wide range of musical instruments. In the back room of the store was a recording studio. It was used to record songs on their label. The songs they sang on the records were big hits in Gospel music. The music company also recorded for individuals who wanted to make a record.

The family consisted of three generations of singers. Hershal Lester (on the far right of the family photo) taught music in one of the high schools in St. Louis. He also drove the luxury bus used for the family's travels to their weekend and holiday appearances.

The entire Lester family loved Botz root beer. After each performance in Clay-

The Lester Family Dynamic Gospel Group

ville, the family headed for an ice-cold bottle of root beer to quench their thirst. The six cases of root beer they took with them only lasted about a week.

The family got tired of so much traveling on the weekends which led them to getting a television program on KSD-TV, a St. Louis station. It was a live gospel show on Sunday mornings. The show was broadcast from inside Meramec Caverns in a large auditorium in the cave where the acoustics were good. The show was on the air for ten years.

The Lester family was invited back to Clayville for many years.

CHAPTER 13

Later at the plant Leon and Leroy had a meeting in the office to figure out their disbursements of their windfall. Many bills were overdue. The most important items were the utilities and taxes (those damn taxes). However, they were able to get their supplies caught up — without them you are dead in the water. The cost of the essential ingredients for making soda were going up. Since Fidel Castro, the regular supply of sugar cane from Cuba dried up. The sugar had to come from Hawaii which was higher priced. The extracts and concentrate for the flavors had gone up. Another problem was the farmer who grew sorghum and made the sorghum into molasses died and the farm was sold. Sorghum molasses is the sweetener used in the root beer. It was the secret ingredient. It gave a smooth yet robust taste that everyone loved. They had to find a new source for sorghum molasses; of course they had to pay more. Another item that squeezed them was the price of gasoline.

It went up to 46 cents a gallon. In a week's time that added up because they delivered to a 75 mile radius around Clayville.

Botz Bottling Company caught up with their bills but the challenge was not over. How could they compete with the big boys? If Coke and Pepsi could sell a can of soda for .15, very few people would buy Botz for .20. They must compete without raising their prices. The commercial Ferlin Husky made ran on the radio for 30 days, four times a day, which boosted sales. Leon and Leroy cut their salaries, since their children were older and could take care of themselves. Their wives got part-time jobs to help out. It was a no win situation. They owed the radio station air time. Leroy wrote the radio station a check for half the amount owed. Greg Allen agreed to let them pay the other half later.

The 60's Had It's Problems

Johnson   Kennedy

Kennedy Stood Up To Kruchev During The Cuban Missle Crisis.

The Couragous And Charismatic President Kennedy Was Assassinated. Johnson Became President. He Chose Not To Run For A Second Term. He Failed To Stop The Vietnam War. His Great Society Program Was Damaged By The Rioting in Watts.

CHAPTER 14

A few weeks later at the office, Leroy asked Leon if he could talk to Linda about a guy she had been seeing.

Leroy said, "It seems that she is in love with one of those hippies. The guy is no good, he is worthless. He has been hanging around town in an old Volkswagen bus and camping out at the old clay mine with a bunch of other hippies. The other day they were protesting the Vietnam War down on the town square and the police made them move on. Linda was right in the middle of it. She was hanging all over that hippie. When I confronted her about it, she was very defiant. She said she loved Charlie because he stands up for the rights of all young people. I know this Charlie has been talking a lot of trash to her. Linda is very smart and can have a great future; I don't want her to ruin it. I don't want to be too protective of her but this can be serious. Linda always thought you were the greatest, and I believe she will listen to you."

Leon agreed to talk to her. Saturday morning Leon took Linda out to breakfast. Leon ordered bacon and eggs then asked Linda what she would like to have. Linda replied, "Anything but eggs. I can't stand eggs and neither can my mother."

Leon smiled but did not say anything as he remembered an old prank that went wrong.

While they were waiting for their food Linda started laughing. Leon asked her why she was laughing. Still laughing Linda said, "I just remembered what you did to Lisa one time when you took all of your nieces out to eat. She had mashed potatoes and gravy on her plate. You made a comment about the radiation coming from her mashed potatoes and told her to hold out her hand and feel. When she did you pushed her hand into the potatoes. Everyone thought that was funny except Lisa. It took her a long time to get over it. She's a lot like dad."

Leon laughed then turned the conversation to a more serious manner.

Leon said, "Linda, I know your father is concerned about your involvement with Charlie. He loves you and so does your entire family. I checked this guy out and he is not working. He did not show up for duty when he was drafted. He will probably get arrested or end up in Canada with the other draft dodgers. Now I can't say his cause is right or wrong. I can see where young people don't want to fight someone else's war. It seems this country is always involved in foreign entanglements. I don't know if it's politics or if it really does any good. My Army Reserves unit was called to serve in Korea. I did not want to go. I was so in love with your aunt Betty, but I felt an obligation and I had to fulfill it. This Charlie has long straggly hair that is unkempt. A beard that is unkempt and his clothes are dirty. If this guy had any self respect he would take care of his appearance. Think of it honey, he is not responsible. This is the greatest country in the world, and we all need the freedom to protest anything we don't believe in. You have studied history, you know the sacrifices that have been made to make this country great and keep it great. Your father and I love you and want a good life for you."

Leon also added that the police chief and one of his men went to the old clay mine to check out the gang of hippies and caught them smoking marijuana. They took it away from them and warned them if they were caught smoking it again they would be arrested. He asked Linda if she ever smoked it. Linda replied. "Yes, but I didn't inhale."

After listening to her uncle, Linda said, "You know Uncle Leon, you are right."

Surprisingly he got through to her.

CHAPTER 15

Uncle Mike's drinking got worse and they needed someone else to help out at the bottling plant.

Uncle Mike never had a family of his own. His only known relative was a brother who died. Mike and his brother were bachelors. Neither of them had ever been married. They lived together for many years. After Mike's brother's death he moved into a boarding house operated by Abigale Martin, an older woman. Everyone called her Abbie. After her husband died, her son and daughter moved east for better paying jobs. Abbie was left alone in a big old house. She decided to take in boarders. Abbie looked after Uncle Mike like a mother. However, when Uncle Mike had too much to drink, she wouldn't let him in. He would have to sleep on the front porch. That was fine in the warmer months. In the bitter cold, she would let him sleep it off on the living room floor by the door.

A dwarf with a clubfoot who happened to be a former preacher lived in the boarding house. He and Uncle Mike did not get along. He saw Uncle Mike as an unrepentant sinner. Uncle Mike came in drunk one night, picked up the dwarf and said, "You little shit, I wonder how far I could throw you?"

The dwarf yelled, "Put me down you no-good sinner, may God help you."

"You little bastard, I'll put you down," replied Uncle Mike. That comment hit deep because the dwarf was a bastard.

Uncle Mike and the dwarf didn't speak again until Uncle Mike was covered in snow and Abbie called the dwarf to help.

One December, there came an early snow. After dark, everyone was off the streets. As the snow continued, Uncle Mike was the only one outside. He staggered his way to Abbie's front porch and sat down near one end, leaned against the house, finished his bottle of Wild Turkey 110 proof whiskey, passed out and fell over. The snow continued. It drifted on to the porch. Mike was soon covered with a blanket of snow. His three-legged dog stayed safe under the porch directly below Mike. When Abbie walked out on the porch to let the cat out, she saw Uncle Mike covered with the white blanket, she cried, "Oh, my goodness." She rushed over and brushed the snow off Mike. His body was steaming. She called the dwarf to help get him inside. When they went to lift him up, he mumbled, "Where is my Wild Turkey." They knew he was still alive.

Abbie called the doctor, he told her to cover Mike up with blankets to keep him warm. He also instructed Abbie to bring Mike to see him first thing in the morning.

The doctor told Mike that the dwarf's quick thinking had saved Mike's life. After that, Uncle Mike and the dwarf became friends. The three-legged dog, Uncle Mike, and the dwarf always hung out. Uncle Mike recovered just fine, except for his feet that were frost bitten. After that he walked with a slight limp. Mike again gave up drinking for two weeks, and life went on in Clayville. Mike and his three-legged dog, and the dwarf continued to limp around town together.

CHAPTER 16

Meanwhile back at the plant, Leon's oldest boy, Lou came to work at the bottling plant. Leon trained Lou on how to operate the bottling machinery and had him study the formula from the notebook that was kept in the small safe in the plant. However, Lou got confused on occasion. One day Leroy came in from a business meeting cutting through the plant. He rushed into the office and exclaimed, "Leon, you had better get out there and see what Lou is doing. It looks like he is making orange cola or something." Leon went out to the plant and confronted Lou.

"Son," he said. "You have to pay attention to what you are doing. We will have to throw away that orange liquid. We can't sell rust colored soda."

Lou said, "Dad, I have no interest in the soda business, and I don't want to struggle in it the way you and Uncle Leroy have."

"What are you interested in son?" asked Leon. "I want to get into aircraft engineering and design," he answered. "There is a good school over in Lynn, Missouri, and I'd like to go there."

"Well, if that is what you really want," answered Leon, "I'll do all I can to get you there."

Leon returned to the office and told Leroy that Lou had no interest in the soda business that there was no use trying to force it on him. "I will come in a couple of evenings a week to do the work he was doing."

Leroy said "Okay, I have something to tell you, while I was out I discovered that Coke passed out a free Coke to all the kids after school. To top that, it was in plastic bottles. I can't believe . . . plastic bottles. I also discovered that Dale at the IGA has a brother-in-law who is a salesman for Coke. His brother-in-law had to be behind the free samples for the kids."

"Damn it!" sputtered Leon." I knew something was up. Now I know why Dale has been so partial to Coke. Well, what are we going to do about it?"

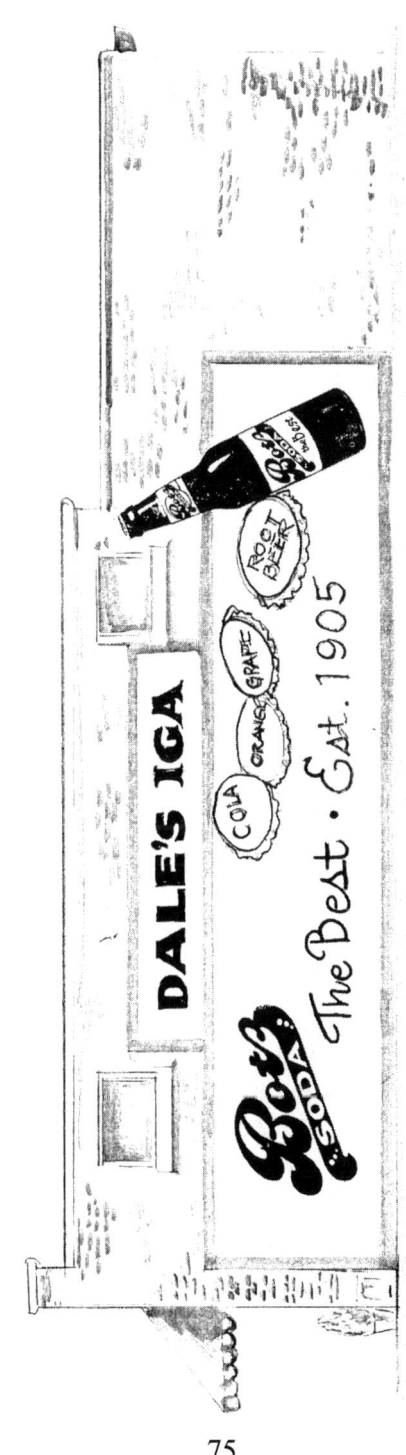

Leroy answered, "We are not going to follow Coke by bribing kids to drink soda."

The old '48 Dodge finally shot craps. It was towed back to the plant and was parked inside. The Botz Soda Company rented a U-Haul to get immediate orders delivered. Leon's pickup and Leroy's station wagon were also used to make deliveries. It was apparent that the engine on the Dodge had to be replaced. They knew it was going to be expensive and, as usual, they were low on money. Leon called in Herman, a crude, greasy, old boy from Arkansas. He was the best mechanic they could find. He showed up greasy as ever to give them a bid.

The three of them were in the office talking about the work that needed to be done on the Dodge. Since they needed the truck and did not have the money to pay the full amount, they asked if they could pay 1/3 now, 1/3 in 30 days and the balance in 60 days.

Herman said to Leroy, "If you hook me up with that cute little wife of yours, I'll do the entire thing for nothing." With a wild, angry look on his face Leroy responded, "You no-good, rotten, grease ball, scumbag!"

Herman said, "Hey, take it easy. I was only kidding."

"Screw you!" answered Leroy. I've seen you looking over my wife in the past."

Leon said, "He knows how sensitive you are about your wife and daughters. He provoked you on purpose. He is just having a little fun with you."

Leroy answered awkwardly, "Maybe I should lighten up a little."

Leroy explained about a situation that happened at the Fourth of July picnic. "I was standing near Linda in the Botz bottle and these two teenage guys were watching the bottle. One of them said they'd like to see what was in the bottle. He got down on his hands and knees and looked up into the bottle and said, 'What a body. I'd like to get me some of that.'

"I clutched my fist and said, 'I'll give you some of this.' It was all I could do to keep from hitting him, the little bastard. It was all I could do to control myself."

Herman said, "Man, I'm sorry." Leroy answered, "Okay, but watch yourself."

"Back to the truck. The engine is out. However, I will take payments and give you a good price."

It was one of those days at the Botz Bottling Company and it wasn't over yet. Leon's wife, Betty, called and spoke in an excited voice. "I can't believe it, Leon. I was at the IGA Store and you know our big wall sign on the side of the store. It was coated out and a Coke sign was painted in its place. Pete painted it."

"Damn it!" exclaimed Leon. "That really burns my ass."

Herman, who was standing nearby, put his hand around his backside, held it about the height of his butt and said, "What really burns my ass is a fire about that high." Then he laughed and laughed. Leon was not amused, "Shut up grease ball and fix my truck," he retorted.

Leon got Pete on the phone. "What the hell are you doing? You stuck a knife in my back."

"Sorry, Leon," said Pete. "You are the best friend I ever had and I think the world of you but I got a real good price for that job. If I didn't do it, they would have gotten a sign painter from Springfield to do it. They paid me C.O.D. A lot of work I've done for you, I never got paid for. I'm not in the favor business. I haven't said much about the money you owe me because I know Botz Bottling Company is struggling."

Leon felt bad about taking advantage of their friendship. Leon said, "Pete, I understand where you are coming from, we'll get you some money soon. We'll eventually get you caught up. I know you have been giving us a break on our signs and we appreciate it."

Pete answered, "Heck, I know you will take care of me eventually." A momentarily strained relationship was mended and life went on at the Botz Bottling Plant.

CHAPTER 17

There was no way Leon was going to let Coke's move at IGA go unanswered. A week later, Leon stopped in at the IGA for a loaf of bread. On his way out, he accidentally on purpose dropped a stink bomb. The smell was so bad it cleared the store. Even Dale, the owner couldn't take it, he had to leave for a short time. A week after that Leon went by the IGA and squirted super glue in the lock of the front door. He left a note on the door reading, "You have been Botz by the best."

Later that morning, Leon got a visit from the police chief. He told Leon that he got a complaint from Dale at IGA. "Criminal charges can be avoided if you knock off the pranks." Leon agreed. No more pranks on Dale or his property.

"I'll knock it off. Dale is a fellow Lion, and I'll pay for the lock."

The chief called Dale and told him that there would be no more pranks. "I got him straightened out. I'm going to bring over a replacement lock in a little while," said the chief.

CHAPTER 18

The last picnic of the season for Botz was Marston Days. It was the town's big Labor Day celebration. The town was coming back from a decaying community. A new aluminum plant was built outside Caruthersville. You could see the plant from Marston. The 200-foot smoke stack and the huge buildings stood along the horizon. It was a boost for the economy of the entire area.

Leon and Pete met at Marston Days. Their visit would not be complete without a prank. Leon cut up a stack of newspaper, put a dollar bill on top rolled up in a bundle to look like a bundle of money, and wrapped a rubber band around it.

Bobby the banker, came to the picnic. Each year he parked in the same spot, away from the other cars. He was afraid someone would scratch the paint on his beloved new car. When the pranksters saw Bobby off in the distance, Pete dropped the bundle near where Bobby parked and then he and Leon blended into the small crowd. They watched Bobby get out of his car, look around, spot the bundle and discreetly pick it up. He got back in his car to open it. He stuck the dollar bill in his pocket and threw the newspaper in a trash can. Pete and Leon stifled their laughter and went to enjoy themselves.

Pete and Leon ran into Bobby about an hour later. Leon said, "Did you spend all that money you found awhile ago?"

Bobby was embarrassed and angry. His face turned red and he said, "You two must think that was funny. Why don't you grow up, you no-good creeps? You'll get yours some day."

Leon said, "Why don't you stop being such a money grabber?"

Botz expected to do well at the celebration. As expected they made a good profit.

CHAPTER 19

The owners of KXBX, Emmett McAuliffe and Johnny Rabbitt showed up to check things out at the station. Emmett asked how the search was going for an announcer. Greg said a kid from Cape Girardeau named Rush Limbaugh came to audition. I asked him what he hoped to achieve at the station. He replied, "Going right to the top. Your job would even do." Greg mentioned how cocky the kid was. "I told him to go back to the boot heel and pick cotton because you will never make it in radio." Rush retorted, "I'm going to California where the real radio stations are and get a job." Johnny mentioned that "some guys with that attitude make it to the top."

They switched gears and Johnny told Greg that he better take care of all old debts.

On Tuesday, Greg Allen from the radio station was knocking on the Botz Bottling Company doors. He wanted the old debt taken care of immediately. He said his partners at the radio station, Johnny Rabbitt and

Emmett McAuliffe wanted the debt paid in full. "I'm really going to be in deep trouble if I don't get this debt taken care of now," he said.

Leon replied, "We can't pay you all of it, but maybe you can have a soda giveaway, a promotion. We will give you 50 cases of free soda pop."

"Well, I don't know about that," said Greg. "I'll have to run it by my partners." Just before he left he said, "Oh by the way, Ferlin Husky has moved to Hawaii."

Leroy replied, "Oh crap! Do you know how much it will cost to send a case of root beer to Hawaii each month?"

CHAPTER 20

The town newspaper came to do a story on Botz Bottling. The newspaper was concerned about the welfare of the town. They did all they could to help the businesses in the town. The paper did a history of the Botz Soda Bottling Company. Leroy furnished a lot of photos and information. Leon and Leroy were the Botz historians. Leon kept small metal signs and cardboard displays. Leroy had the original horse-drawn delivery wagon and their first delivery truck from 1929. He stored everything at his wife Shelly's parent's farm in a big barn. He set the truck up on blocks, wrapped the engine in plastic and rubbed the entire truck down with motor oil to protect it. He covered both the truck and wagon tightly with tarps. He also kept a lot of old root beer kegs and had a collection of original Botz bottles.

When the article was published in the paper, it helped sales a little. However, the biggest draw was the antiques mentioned in the article. Collectors started calling and stopping by the company. Leroy told them nothing was for sale. "I'm passing everything on to my family."

CHAPTER 21

Leon had been listening to a motivational tape by Earl Nightingale and Zig Zigler. The message was — "If you believe in yourself, you can make it happen. What can be conceived and believed can be achieved. Play your own hunches. Don't worry about negative feedback and criticism." That's why he didn't tell Leroy his plan. Leon figured a new product to keep up with the times was needed. He had the formula figured out. Pineapple-Orange juice loaded with caffeine.

Leon discussed his new idea with Pete. Leon said, "You know that bulletin board of yours at the entrance of town, you have a blank side. Will you do just one more favor for me? This will turn our entire soda business around." Things were slowing down for Pete. So he painted the sign over the weekend. Bright and early Monday morning the calls started coming in to the company. Leroy had no knowledge of the sign.

All the leaders of the churches in town called. The calls went something like this, "What you are doing is totally sacrilegious. It's blasphemy!" Leroy confronted Leon as he walked in. "What the hell is going on with the sign?"

Leon answered, "It's a new idea for a new beverage." The sign says, "New from Botz bottling — Jesus Juice — It Lifts Your Spirits." Leroy shouted, "What were you thinking?"

Leon replied, "Don't you know Jesus is big now. A lot of our youth are Jesus fans." Leroy responded, "One of these days I'm going to knock you on your ass! All the churches in town are up in arms. If we put something like that out, our business will be ruined."

Leon said, "I'm trying to turn this company around."

Leroy told Leon the bad news. "The company is behind in state and federal taxes. We are being hit with penalties and interest. We can't go on operating in the red. Even if we borrow money, we would have to pay that back and that will just add to the strain."

Leon agreed that they couldn't go on like that.

Leroy said, "I'm going to see Mother. She gets a full report from our accountant each month."

Leroy went to his mother's house to discuss the soda business. When he arrived he said, "Hello, Mother."

She answered, "Never mind the Mother stuff, lets get down to business."

They discussed the financial problems of Botz Bottling Company. Lillian said, "We'll have to consider liquidation and other options. Let me sleep on the matter. You and Leon come over tomorrow at 7:00 tomorrow night. We'll figure it all out then."

Leroy said, "Before I go, I have a question. I have always wondered why I often got a whipping when Leon blamed his pranks on me. You never listened to me when I tried to explain the truth."

"You want to know why," explained Lillian. "I don't like you. You are my son and

I love you, but you remind me of your father. You look like him and you act like him. I loved your father, but sometimes I could not stand him. You have that same pompous attitude as him. He always called me Mother and you call me Mother. I don't like to be called Mother. I never said anything to him about it because I loved him and that was what he liked to call me, I accepted it. I guess I took my anger out on you. I'm very sorry for that. Leon always calls me Mom. I like that. He is always laughing and pleasant."

Lillian could see that Leroy was hurt and felt bad. She said, "Son, I love you very much and I am proud of you, your brother, and your sister, that comes from my heart." They hugged each other and Leroy left.

CHAPTER 22

Leon and Leroy arrived at their mother's house promptly at 7:00 the next evening. Lillian was now in her late nineties and in failing health. However, she still had a sharp mind. Lillian announced that the three of them had some serious decisions to make.

"I have decided to liquidate," announced Lillian. "I know I promised your father we would keep Botz Bottling Company operating, but times have changed, things have changed, and circumstances change. I'm sure he would understand and back my decision. Why beat a dead horse? I know you boys have been trying very hard to keep the business alive. I am very proud of you both. I've been watching the business very closely while letting you handle the operation of the plant. I did not want to interfere. You boys know how to run the plant. I have put out some feelers about selling the business, but no one wants to come up with any serious money. Liquidating is the best way to go. I figured getting rid of everything, including the truck would be a wise decision. We'll sell this house, the plant, the building, and the machinery. I also suggest you sell the farm. This will take care of all debts and give you boys enough money to get into something else. Lou Ann has been wanting me to go to Los Angeles and live with her ever since your father died. This house is way too big for one person, and I have a hard time getting around. I don't want a full-time nurse taking care of me. This house would be great for a large growing family. You kids were raised here, the house was plenty big enough and it's been well kept." Lillian paused to give the boys a chance to digest what she had just told them then added, "Do you boys have any problems with my plan?"

They both reluctantly agreed that her plan was the best solution. Leroy did not like the idea of getting rid of the antiques, but then figured they would just be sold after he was dead anyway.

The parents of Leroy's wife Shelly, left their farm to the Botz families in their will. When they were alive, both families took good care of them and were always there when they needed them.

Lillian told Leon and Leroy to go over to Tom Tetlow's Real Estate office and make arrangements to sell the property. Mrs. Tetlow had retired from teaching but Mr. Tetlow was still running his business. Tom stuttered but was a good businessman who knew what he was doing. Before going to Tetlow's Real Estate office Leroy gave Leon strict advice about his conduct while in the office.

When Mr. Tetlow answered the phone he said, "Hel . . . hell . . .o, Th . . . this is T . . . T . . . Tom Tet . . . Tet . . . Tit . . . Tetlow." Mr. Tetlow listed the property immediately. He already had a prospective buyer for Lillian's house and had connections with a group that bought and sold farms. Leroy got back with a few people who were interested in the 1929 truck and wagon. There was a collector who wanted all of the Botz memorabilia and old signs, posters, and displays. He was also very interested in the Botz dancing bottle.

The Botz brothers were in the process of shutting down the plant. The bottling machinery went to Fitz's Root Beer. They had a restaurant in their plant. People could watch the soda being bottled while they ate. Fitz's had plans to open another restaurant. The bottling plant would be surrounded on all four sides with eating for patrons. The plant would be surrounded by glass. Fitz's made a deal with Botz to buy their bottling equipment. The change was to take place in three weeks. Leon and Leroy made plans to make one last run of their cola and keep the last soda off the line. Leroy was to give it to his youngest daughter to keep as a family heirloom. They would store the last case of soda pop.

CHAPTER 23

Leroy bargained with a very wealthy man who wanted to buy his entire Botz collection. Leroy got a good price for his collection.

Leon and Leroy had arranged to meet the man who wanted to buy the truck and wagon stored at the farm. As they left town on the blacktop country road, neither of them said a word. It was a warm, still, October day. The leaves had changed to hues of red and gold. It was a beautiful sight to see the rolling hills. They seemed to say that summer was over and autumn had arrived. Just as their drive was saying their lives were changing forever. They had an empty feeling as they thought it over. They knew it was all over for them. They drove in silence the whole way to the farm. The buyer got out of his Mercedes and walked over to greet the brothers.

The Botz brothers took the wrap off the truck and wagon. The buyer was amazed at the condition of them. Leroy told him that the truck still ran and everything was in work-

*The Botz First Delivery Truck.
It Replaced The Horse Drawn Wagons.
Two Other Trucks Followed Soon.*

ing order when he put it in storage. "I was a little boy when Dad had to take it off the road because it was too slow; it was geared low to carry a heavy load. The top speed was about 15 miles per hour." The multi-millionaire was extremely excited. He told Leroy to name his price. The man gave the brothers $100,000 for the truck and $50,000 for the wagon.

On the way home Leroy said, "The Boylan Bottle works has been in business since 1891; they are still using the same glass bottles as we were, yet they are still making it and we did not. They are up in New Jersey. I guess they have a bigger market in the east. Look at all the soda companies that have gone out of business in the last six years. The Missouri Bottleers Association used to have over 40 members, now there are only 11. In Valley Park the Spolker Soda Company gave it up. In St. Charles, the Big Boy Soda Company closed. In St. Louis, Blue Ridge, Bubble Up, Gargers, Dad's Root Beer, and a few others. But the Vess Cola Company is still going strong."

Leon said, "Forget it. It's over for us."

Leroy responded, "Like Mom said, why beat a dead horse."

Leon couldn't believe his ears. "You called her mom."

Leroy said, "She likes that better. Well it looks like we are going to come out of this in good shape, even after we pay our debts."

Lillian's house sold at above market value. The plant building was sold to a chain lumber company. The root beer formula was sold to Pepo, a large food and beverage conglomerate. The farm was sold to an oil tycoon from Saudi Arabia. Tom Tetlow did a great job. He got top dollar for all the properties.

After everything was sold, and all debts were paid, the Botz family had close to a million to split. All their money was deposited in Bobby's bank, which made him very happy. He even started to like Leon.

What were the Botz brothers going to do next? Well, Leroy bought the IGA store from Dale. His family would run that business. And, believe it or not, Leon bought a Coke route. "If you can't beat the big boys, join them."

CHAPTER 24

Leon and Leroy went down to the plant to make their last soda pop run. The equipment was going to be gone next week. Leroy was standing at the end of the line. Leon walked up the line a little ways to check things out. He walked up to where Leroy was standing. When the last bottle got to the end of the line the contents was an amber color.

"You pissed in it!" Leroy shouted. He turned and hit Leon in the jaw knocking him on his ass. Leon went tumbling back over some five-gallon cans.

He got up, holding his jaw and laughing. "I can't believe it. You finally did it. You knocked me on my ass."

Leroy grabbed the bottle and threw it against the wall, shattering the bottle and spewing its contents everywhere. Leroy took the next bottle and said, "This is the last soda pop."

Leroy has a mean streak that seldom came out. Leon just could not let the moment pass. He began to sing, "Bad, bad, Leroy Botz. The meanest man in the whole damn town . . . " They both laughed and laughed as they hosed off the equipment and floor. They solemnly locked the door for the last time.

Leon was not finished yet. The next day he drove around the town square in his new bright yellow Coca-Cola delivery truck blowing a huge air horn. And that is the story of the last soda pop.

It's true, it's fiction.

It's real, it's unreal.

"If you can't beat the big boys, join them."

-Leon Botz